Old MacDonald
had some
Cows

Written by Nicola Baxter
Illustrated by Caroline Davis

Bright ☆ Sparks

MERRY CHRISTMAS
TO HEATHER
FROM
GRANNY SAUCHIE
XX

Old MacDonald had a farm and on that farm he had some COWS...

The new arrival

All day long, Old MacDonald's cows grazed in the green meadow. As they munched, they chatted. Nothing much happened on the farm that Poppy, Annabel, Emily and Heather didn't know about.

One morning, Poppy was munching near the hedge, when Old MacDonald came to visit the horses in the field next door.

"Here's an apple for you, Tilly," he said, "and one for you, George. I wanted you to be the first to hear – we're expecting a new baby on the farm. You can imagine how excited Mrs MacDonald is about it because…"

But before he could finish, there came the sound of thundering hooves, as a cow, bursting with news, dashed off to find her friends.

"Are you sure?" mooed Annabel, as Poppy panted out what she had heard.

"Positive," gasped Poppy.

"Old MacDonald and Mrs MacDonald, aren't they, well, a bit old to be having a baby?" asked Emily.

"Yes, I thought that," said Poppy. "But I heard it from Old MacDonald himself."

"But if Mrs MacDonald has a baby to look after," said Heather, "who will give me my beauty treatments before the County Show? I simply must win a rosette again this year."

There was complete silence. Then Annabel said what they had all been thinking.

"Ladies! This news is far too important to keep to ourselves! We must tell the others immediately!" And off the four cows dashed.

So Emily leaned over the gate and mumbled in Jenny the hen's ear. "*What*?" she squawked. "If Mrs MacDonald has a baby to look after, who will collect my eggs? I must tell Henry!"

Henry the cockerel crowed when he heard the news. "*Well, cock-a-doodle-doo!*" he cried. "If Mrs MacDonald has a baby to look after, who will throw me my corn to peck?" So Henry hurried off to talk to Debbie the duck.

And so it went on. Debbie told Milly the cat. Milly told Percy the pig. Percy told Bruce the sheepdog. And Bruce scampered off to tell Maria and the rest of the sheep.

By lunch time, every animal on the farm was worried. Things simply wouldn't be the same if Mrs MacDonald was looking after a baby. In fact, the animals were all so busy and bothered, they didn't notice a truck pulling into the farmyard.

"The new arrival!" called Old MacDonald.

"What, already?" squawked Jenny. "But I thought… oh!"

Out of the truck trotted a beautiful little foal, a new friend for Tilly and Old George.

"It's so lovely to have another baby animal on the farm!" cried Mrs MacDonald.

She was too excited to hear the sigh of relief from all the animals, or the mooing from the meadow, as the other cows had a few well-chosen words with Poppy!

Moo! Moo! Moo!

The Meadow Ladies Chorus,
Is something rather new.
You'll hear them all too clearly,
They're singing **"Moo! Moo! Moo!"**

They try to trill like budgies,
And copy blackbirds, too.
The only song they really know,
Of course, is **"Moo! Moo! Moo!"**

They practise in the morning,
And in the nighttime, too.
It doesn't make a difference though,
They still sing **"Moo! Moo! Moo!"**

In Old MacDonald's Farmyard,
You'll hear pigs oinking, too.
But louder still the ladies sing,
"Moo, Moo! Moo, Moo! Moo, Moo!"

A hat like that!

Heather the cow took great care of her appearance. No cow on the farm had such shiny hooves or such a glossy coat. She had already won three rosettes at the County Show, and she wanted to win more.

One windy afternoon, Heather was sheltering near a hedge. You can imagine her surprise when she found a beautiful straw hat on a branch. It did have a couple of holes in it, but after all, an elegant cow has to put her ears somewhere!

She strolled back across the field with her nose in the air, and the hat placed firmly on her head. Heather couldn't wait to show it off to her friends.

But Poppy, Annabel and Emily simply carried on munching. Heather tried a tiny lady-like cough. The munching didn't stop for a second. So Heather coughed a little louder. The munching grew louder.

Finally, Heather couldn't bear it any longer. "Haven't you noticed anything?" she mooed.

"Did someone say something?" asked Emily.

"It was me!" cried Heather, tossing her head.

"Oh, so it was," said Annabel, returning to a particularly juicy clump of green grass.

"I'm feeling rather sleepy, I think I'll just have a little snooze," said Poppy.

"And I'm going for a walk," said Emily.

Heather was not a patient cow.

"Look at my hat!"

Of course, the other cows had noticed the hat, but they loved to tease their friend.

"I always think," said Poppy, "that hats are rather… old-fashioned."

"Nonsense," Heather replied. "Only the most fashionable cows are wearing them."

"It's new then, is it?" asked Annabel.

"Certainly!" Heather replied. "It's the very latest style."

"Didn't Mrs MacDonald have a hat like that a few years ago?" asked Emily.

"I don't think so!" Heather said firmly. "Mrs MacDonald is lovely, but she's not what you would call stylish. Only a prize-winning cow could carry off a hat like this."

"If you say so, dear," mooed Annabel.

That evening, the cows ambled into the farmyard as usual to be milked. Before long, all the other animals had gathered round.

"They're admiring my hat!" whispered Heather to Poppy.

But the giggling and chuckling didn't sound like animals who thought Heather looked beautiful. It sounded more like animals who thought she looked rather silly.

"So that's what happened to Scarecrow Sam's hat!"

cried Old MacDonald.

Nowadays, when Heather starts putting on her airs and graces, Poppy, Emily and Annabel know just what to do – talk turns from ears and horns to hats, and Heather tiptoes away.

Old MacDonald had a farm,
E-I-E-I-O!

And on that farm he had some cows,
E-I-E-I-O!
With a moo, moo here
And a moo, moo there.
Here a moo,
There a moo,
Everywhere a moo, moo!
Old MacDonald had a farm,
E-I-E-I-O!

And on that farm he had some horses,
With a neigh, neigh here...

And on that farm he had some ducks,
With a quack, quack here...

And on that farm he had a tractor,
With a brum, brum here...

Nibbling neighbours

One sunny morning in the meadow, Annabel was happily munching grass when she was surprised to discover a hole where there should be grass. "My dears," she mooed, "there's a hole in our field!"

There was no doubt about it. Someone had dug a large, round, deep hole in the ground.

"We must be careful not to fall into it," said Poppy, anxiously.

But the next morning, where there had been one hole before, now there were five! "If this goes on," said Poppy, "we'll have nowhere to stand at all!"

"And nothing to eat," added Emily in alarm.

By the end of the week, there were over a hundred holes dotted around the meadow.

"You've got some nibbling neighbours," said Old MacDonald. "It looks like a family of rabbits has come to stay."

The cows shuddered. "Those little hopping things with long ears?" said Heather. "How can I look my best with them around?"

"And they have very, very large families," warned Emily. "Not just one baby at a time, like cows do."

"It's odd we've never seen one," said Poppy thoughtfully. "Maybe they do their digging in the dark. I'm going to keep watch tonight."

So, that night, as the full moon rose over the meadow, Poppy pretended to go to sleep.

And although she was expecting it, she was still shocked when two bright little eyes and a twitchy nose popped up right in front of her.

"Aaaaaghh!"

cried Poppy.

"Aaaaaghh!"

cried the rabbit, as it disappeared down its hole as fast as it had come.

"You should have followed it!" said Annabel, who had been woken by the noise.

"Down a rabbit hole?" gasped Emily. "Don't be silly, Annabel. She's far too big!"

"Then we're doomed," said Heather, gloomily. "Those rabbits will take over without us even seeing them do it."

The next morning, the cows awoke to an amazing sight. Hundreds of rabbits were sitting all around them.

"Excuse me!" said the largest one. "We have come to ask for your help."

"Help?" echoed Annabel. "We're the ones who need help!"

The rabbit said that his family lived in fear. "Your hooves are so big," he explained, "you could stamp on us without noticing."

Just then, Poppy had one of her excellent ideas. "You would be much safer," she said, "if you lived under the hedgerow."

It worked perfectly. All day in the meadow, there is munching, mooing and mumbling. All night in the hedgerow, there is nibbling, digging and wiggling. And *everyone* is happy.

This is a Bright Sparks Book
This edition published in 2000
Bright Sparks, Queen Street House, 4 Queen Street, Bath BA1 1HE, UK

Copyright © PARRAGON 2000

Created and produced by THE COMPLETE WORKS,
St. Mary's Road, Royal Leamington Spa, Warwickshire CV31 1JP, UK
The Complete Works would like to thank Ellie for all of her help.

ISBN 1-84250-087-2

Printed in China